SEAN AND THE BOOK CURES

THE GREAT SACRIFICE...
CAN YOU SPARE A KIDNEY?

BY:

CHANTE THOMAS

ILLUSTRATED BY:

SAMIULLAH SAHITO

Dear Lewis Family,

Your courage and love for one another is amazing. The grace and courage you displayed makes your journey so beautiful and easy to tell.

Love,
Chante

Dear Sean and Chase,

Reading is a beautiful gift. This is your superpower. Read on and tell the world everything you've learned.

Love,
Your mom

As long as Sean could remember

he loved books!

He loved the smell of them, the

feel of them, the words inside

of them, the picture and the stories

they tell.

As Sean grew older, he would help

others with facts learned from his books.

Little did he know where his

reading journey would take him.

September 2022

What???!!!! No way, that did not happen! Mom, can you explain this to me again? How could someone do that? I'll bet you're wondering why I'm so excited, grab your cup of hot chocolate and settle in. This story will take some time.

Earlier This Year

I met my cousin at the community park to shoot some hoops.

I took a quick run around the track to warm up. I still love to run,

but basketball is one of my favorite sports now. "What's up cousin?"

There was Blake, smiling, with his basketball in hand, ready to play ball.

"You ready to start school?" he asked. I just nodded, but what I really wanted

to do was work on my jump shot. Summer was almost over.

A few hours later, we were done. Tired and exhausted Blake asked me if I wanted to come home with him for dinner. My auntie was the best cook, besides my mom, so of course I said yes. I had to text my mom first to make sure it was okay with her.

Auntie Wen was waiting at the kitchen table with the twins, Kenley

and Kelsey, when we ran into the house. "Hi guys!" She was always enthusiastic,

but today she seemed a little tired. "What's up guys? I made our favorite

dinner tonight, Papa Joe's Pizza.." She said with a wink and a smile. I didn't

get the joke until I heard the pizza delivery driver ring the doorbell.

I guess Auntie Wen wasn't cooking tonight. After dinner, I went home and

began to think about the first day of school. My cousin Tommy told me to

remember to smile on my first day. I thought about him and

promised myself that it would be a great school year.

I was so excited to begin my new school. Leaving behind my crew since kindergarten was tough at first, but my cousin Blake was gonna be in my new class. We arranged this with the counselor so I wouldn't feel alone. Blake was amazing at school! He was super cool, an athlete, smart and the girls liked him too. Who better to show me the ropes at Green Middle School (GMS)?

GMS was the coolest school! It has clubs for everyone and every interest. There was the Green Dolphin Swim Team, The Lego Lovers Club, Young Author's Write, The Rubiks Cubers and, my favorite, Bubbling Over With Science. Blake and I belonged to everything sports related, but you know I love to read, so I decided to start a book club.

A Club is Born

Blake and I were discussing the book club one day and he asked me if we could research books about kidney failure. I have some personal rules that I need to tell you about. My first rule is I work hard and play hard.

Rule number two is sometimes you just have

to be silent. So, thinking about rule number two, I did

not ask any questions, I just nodded (yes) enthusiastically.

Blake and I would meet and read after basketball practice.

He was a voracious reader, kind of like me. You know, I started reading at age

one and researching at age two? We made a list of questions we wanted to

research. What does a kidney do? Do we need both kidneys? What happens

when a kidney doesn't work well anymore? Who fixes kidneys? How do they

fix bad kidneys? Most importantly, can people die if their kidney

stops working?

1) what does a kidney do?
2) Do we need both kidneys?
3) what happens when a kidney does not work well anymore??

The Research

Blake and I got started on our list right away. We created a doc that allowed us to write our research and ideas down at the same time.

I researched question one.

What does a kidney do?

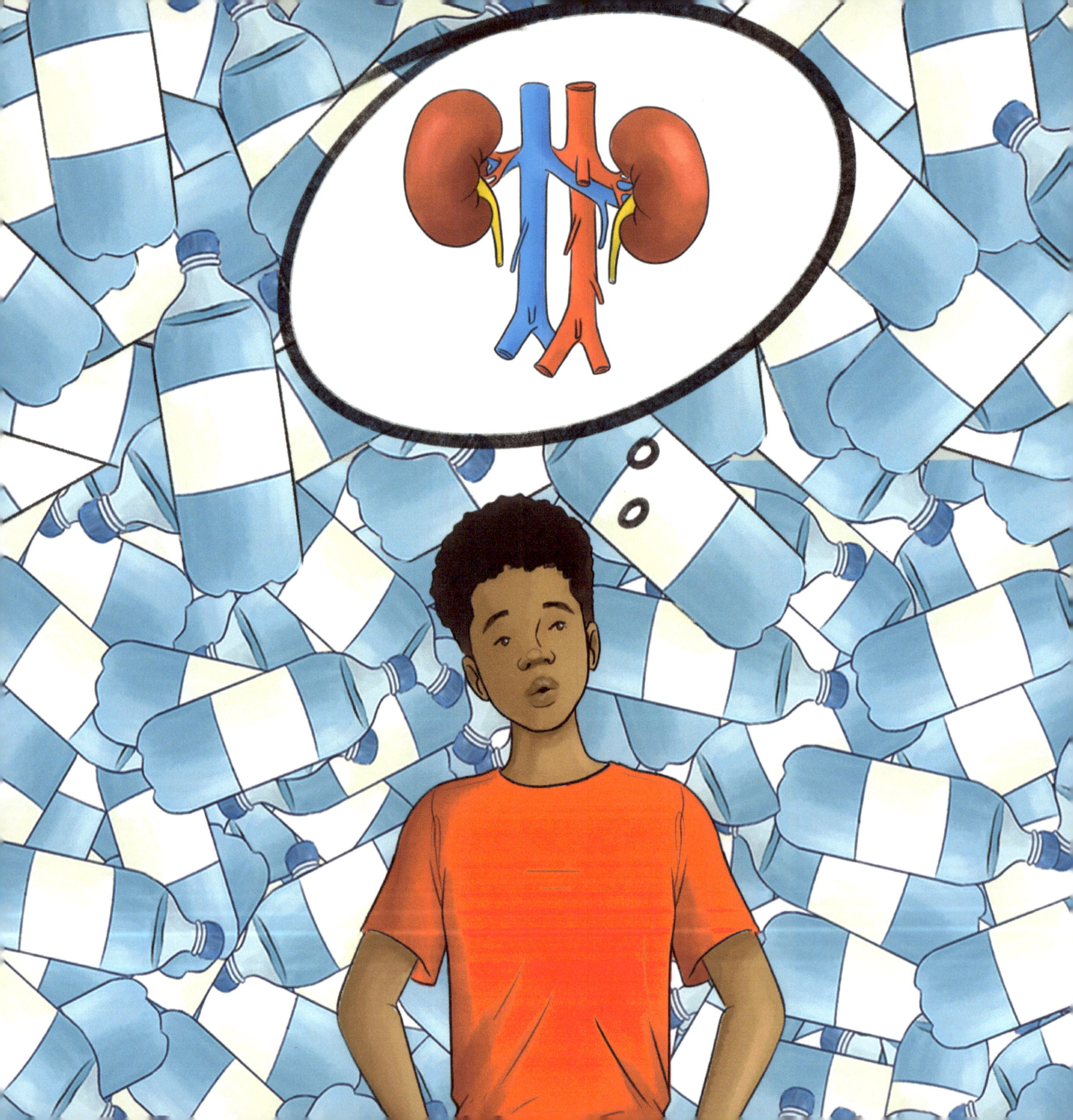

Question 1

What does a kidney do?

The main job of kidneys is to clean the blood from bad stuff called toxins and turn the waste into urine.

Blake added to our notes. We have two kidneys that weigh about 160 grams. They can filter about 200 liters of fluid every 24 hours. What!!? That's like 100 bottles of 2-liter pops???

When we found facts like this, we were totally amazed.

We were becoming awesome researchers.

We met after school and read articles for what seemed like the entire school year. We tried to make our answers sound like it was our own words, I remember Ms. G. telling the class we had to paraphrase when researching.

Question 2

What happens when a kidney doesn't work well anymore?

Blake and I added details to this question. So many things can happen when kidneys are not functioning properly. Harmful toxins and excess fluids can build up into the body. If the fluids don't leave, then it could look like kidney failure. Symptoms of kidney failure are high blood pressure, extreme tiredness, headaches, swelling in the face or ankles, fluid retention and lower back pain.

Question 3

Do we need both kidneys? Blake took the lead on this one.

It is possible to live a healthy and active life with only one functioning kidney.

Phew! That's cool Blake thought.

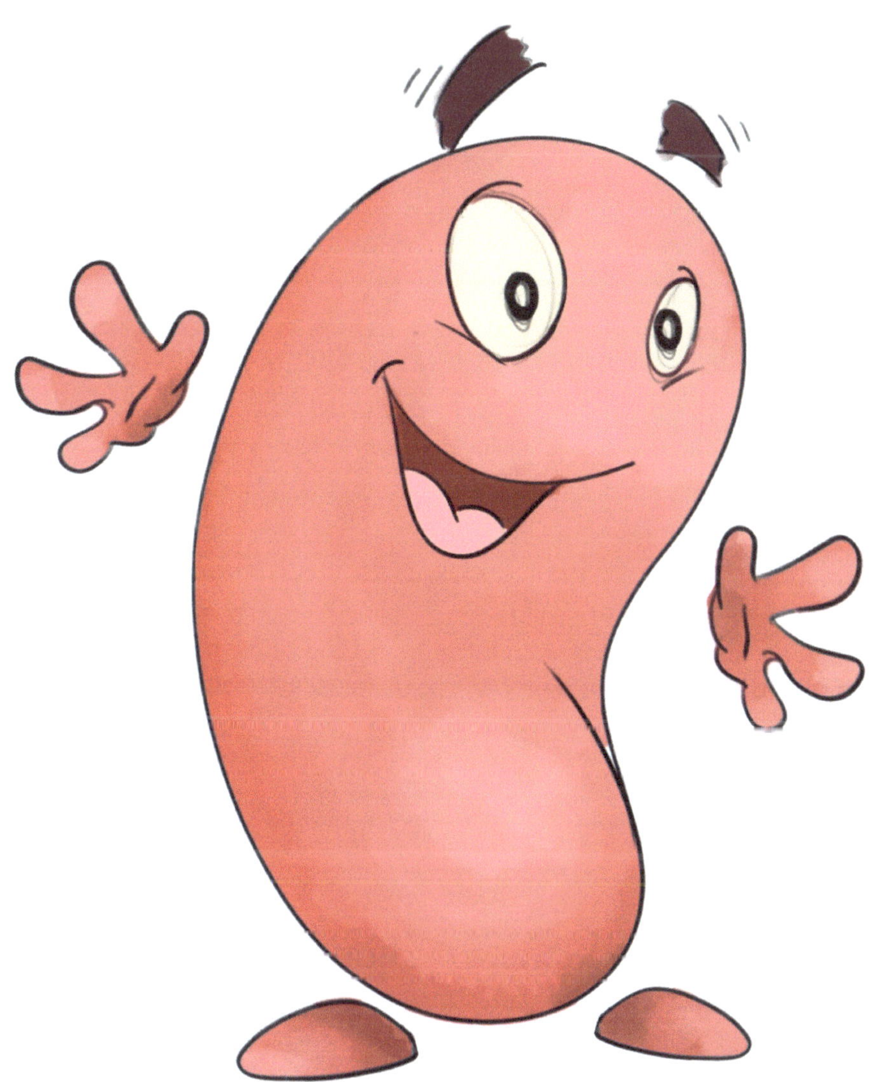

Question 4

Who fixes kidneys?

A special doctor called a nephrologist.

They specialize in the care and function of kidneys.

They treat the diseases of the kidney.

Question 5

How do they fix bad kidneys?

Dialysis can help the body clean the toxins out of the blood.

Some medicines can be prescribed to treat the symptoms of kidney failure.

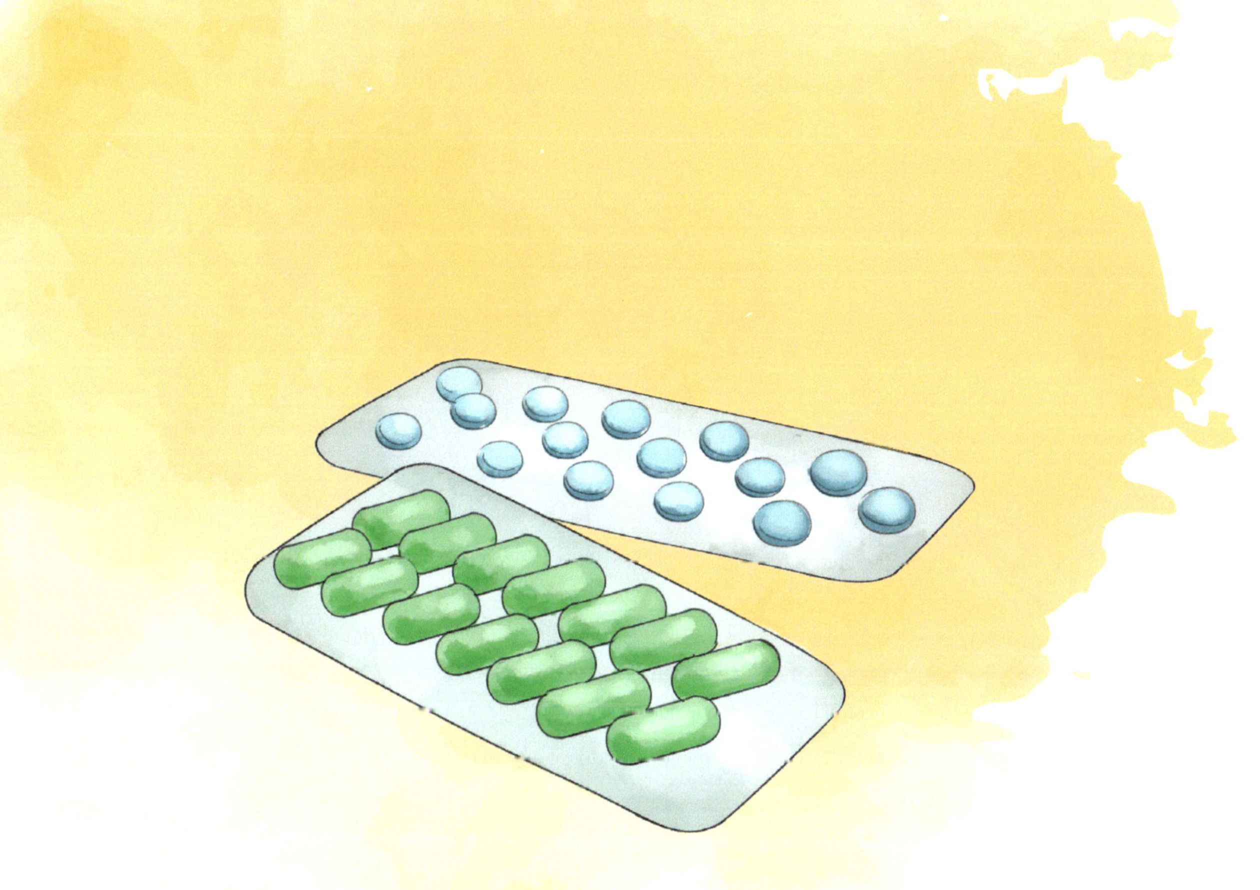

Question 6

Can people die if their kidneys stop working?

Possibly, at the end stage of kidney disease.

Did we really get to the end of our research? It took several months to answer our questions but I still wanted to know more.

Why should people have to die or spend the rest of their life on dialysis? I was sitting alone in my thoughts when Kenley and Kelsey appeared.

"You look real intense Sean, what's up?" Kenley asked. I told the girls that I had been researching kidney disease but I still had a lot of questions.

They gave each other a strange look, then Kelsey said "go talk to a doctor.

Maybe he or she can give you some answers." "That's a great idea!" I couldn't

wait to tell Blake about this.

I heard about a doctor who helps people with kidney disease.

Maybe he would talk to us and tell us how we can help.

We made an appointment with Dr. Steven Lynn. We were able to see him right away. Dr. Lynn was taller than I expected. He had straight black hair, a little gray at the temples and a very kind smile. He told us he used to play basketball in college. His athletic talents provided him a full scholarship to college.

Anyway, with the small talk finished, Blake got right to the point of our visit. "Will organ transplants help people suffering from kidney failure get better?" I looked at him with a little surprised look on my face. We hadn't discussed this question. Again, I remembered my personal rule number two and I chose to stay quiet.

Dr. Lynn stared at both of us intently and then he began to speak.

"Organ donation saves lives. If a patient is a good candidate for an organ transplant, then he or she could add the new kidney surgically and it will clean the blood and help the patient's body resume normal functions."

And then it was Blake's turn….

"Why are so many people suffering from kidney problems? I read that nearly one hundred thousand people are waiting for organ transplants. Why aren't people helping? Is it safe? Can I donate an organ?"

Blake looked pretty anxious as he waited for the answers to his questions.

Kidney
organs
organ donation!
Kidney
operat
onati

Dr. Lynn began to break this down for us. "We need people to volunteer to be organ donors. Sometimes something happens and a person dies and they planned in advance to provide their organs at their passing to people that need them. The more popular organ donation comes from living donors who are in a donor bank and are called upon at the time that they appear to be a good match."

Its a Match….!!!!

"The transplant surgery can only be done after a lot of testing to make sure

there is a strong chance the recipient's body will accept the donated organ.

We really need people of color to get on the donor registries.

I know some people are scared to do this, but organ donation saves lives.

Blake, sometimes there are youth donors but only in very special and unique

medical cases."

Blake took a deep breath and began to reveal a personal story to me

and Dr. Lynn.

Blake's Story

"My mom has been sick for a while. She never complains but I can see her energy is fading. One day I noticed a device on her waist and I asked her about it. Reluctantly she began to tell me everything. Her kidney was failing and she needed to do dialysis to keep her body healthy. My mom was sick from an infection many years ago and had to get a kidney transplant then. Her cousin was an excellent match. She had this kidney for twenty years. Now, she needs a new kidney."

"She is on the transplant list at several hospitals

in different states. She's been waiting and praying. So many family members

have been tested to see if they are a match, but no luck yet.

My dad is now trying to see if he can give mommy a kidney.

If more people would become organ donors, they could help people just

like my mom."

"Your mom sounds really strong," said Dr. Lynn. "Just like your mom's cousin

was able to help her, someone else will be a match too.

It is so important that we have organ donors and we help spread the message

about the need for people of color to be in this pool. I'm so glad you

came to me today and I want you to stay in touch with me."

We thanked Dr. Lynn and rode home in silence.

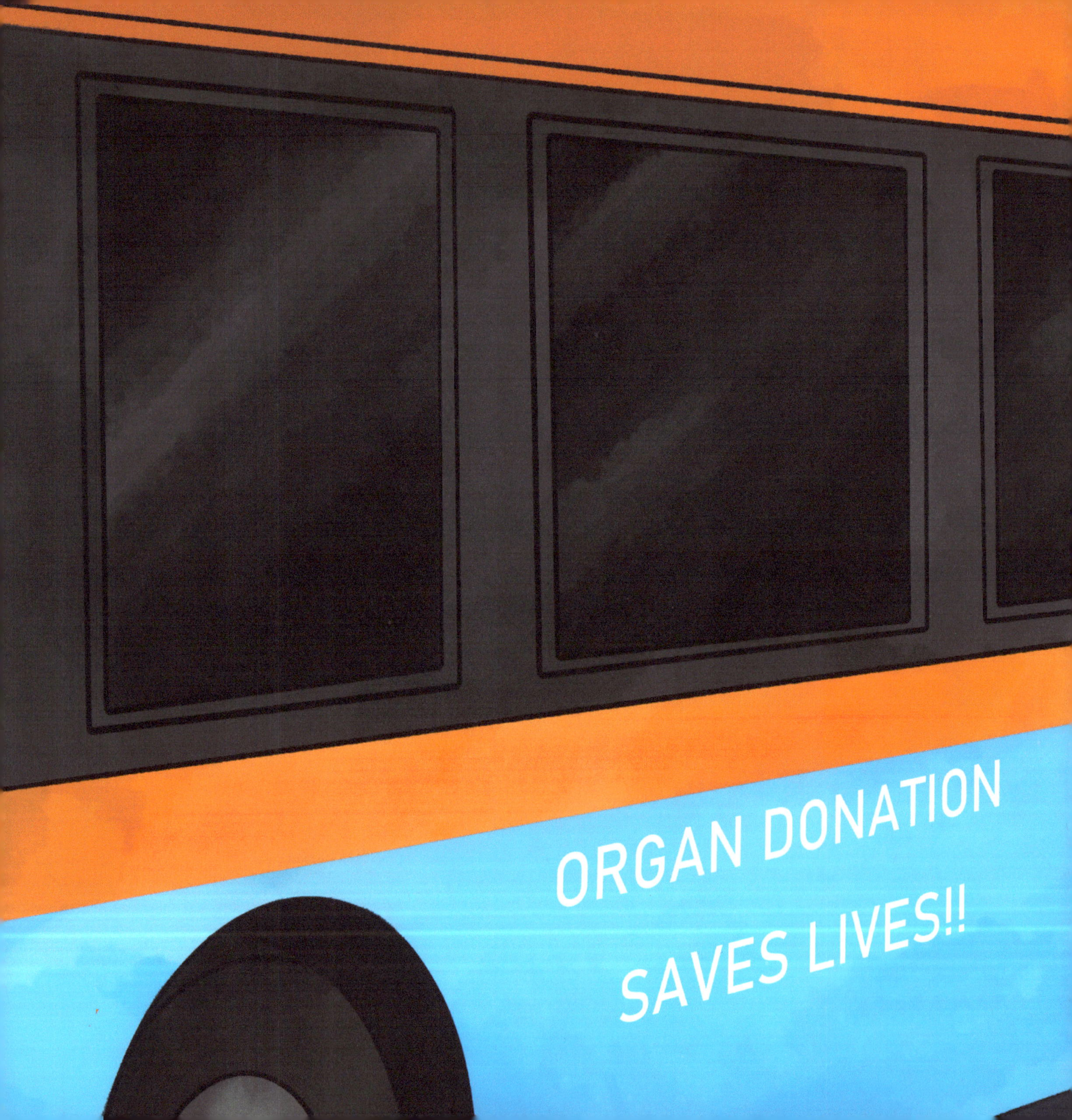
ORGAN DONATION
SAVES LIVES!!

BUS STOP

Finally, I asked if there was anything I could do. Blake said

researching with him was the best thing ever.

He didn't feel so scared and helpless.

Little did I know how important it was that I agreed

to research with Blake at the beginning of the school year.

Quiet

I don't ask Blake too much about his mom and what's going on, but I am

always hoping that she will get a new kidney soon.

Back to the beginning...

"What???!!!! Mom, can you explain this to me again? How could

someone do that?"

"Auntie Wen got a new kidney. Uncle G was a match. It took two

years of testing, praying, looking at the different donation programs,

but finally a hospital agreed that this would work. Uncle G was an

approved match and could give Auntie Wen one of his

kidneys," mom explained.

Mommy! That is a huge sacrifice, I couldn't believe Uncle G gave his

kidney to Auntie. He was so brave to do that. After all our research

and everything we learned, this I know for sure, Auntie Wen is a

living miracle. I was so happy for her but I wondered about how

they were doing. She showed me a picture of the two of them in the

hospital grinning from ear to ear. I knew everything would be

alright.

I ran to my room and called Blake. This was the best day ever! Blake told me

his mom was feeling so much better. The new kidney immediately began

cleansing her blood and she is getting stronger everyday. "Sean, our research

took away my scared feelings. I hope we can help someone else with our

story."

Sean's Personal Rules to Live By…

1) Work Hard and Play Hard

2) Sometimes, you just have to be silent

3) Don't be afraid to ask for help

4) Organ donation is an act of love

Chante Thomas, is a twenty-seven year veteran teacher in Shaker Heights, and has been writing

children's stories over the span of her career. She is an active member of the Shaker Heights Teacher's

Association, Cleveland Chapter of the Chums, Inc., Jack and Jill of America and Alpha Kappa Alpha Sorority,

Incorporated. She is the mother of two sons, ages twelve and nine, and a caregiver to her eighty-eight year old mother.

In 2018, she decided it was time to bring her stories to life and published her first book, *Where I'm From*.

This book tells the geographic story of five diverse children with roots in the United States, Africa and Asia.

She has continued to write a second book, *Go To School Tommy* and her third book, *Sean and the Book Cures*.

Author Chante Thomas desires to inspire youth to read, create and write stories stemming from their own experiences.

Epilogue

This beautiful story is a fictional account of a real miracle.

From Wendy Lewis...

My family is so grateful for the courageous and innovative doctors who have worked tirelessly to support my medical journey. I came together successfully with my family, friends and doctors to have two successful kidney transplants. This is a situation of hope and faith, not despair. If you know anyone who is suffering from kidney disease, tell them our story.

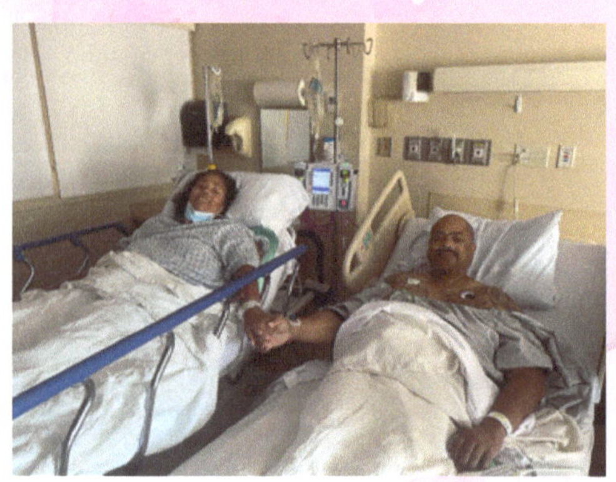
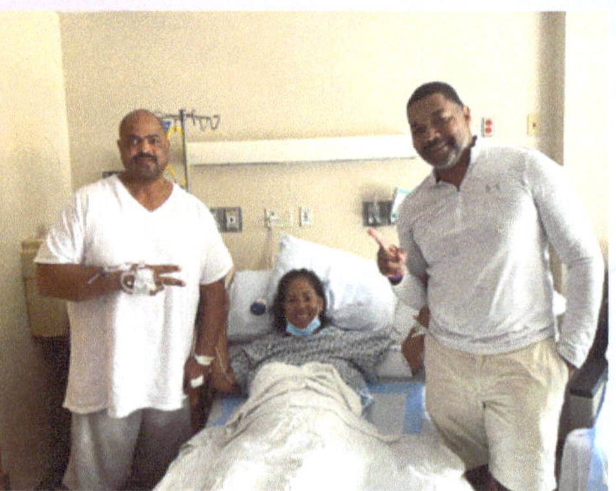

Wendy and husband,Greg Lewis, and Cousin Clifford DeFoor,the first donor.